Elephant Walk

Jean Craighead George

Illustrated by Anna Vojtech

Disney
PRESS

New York

Just as the sun came up, Silver Tusk, the matriarch of the Wamba Elephant Family, lifted her trunk and smelled the breeze. A wafted odor startled her. She raised her ears and flapped them against her neck and shoulders. They made a sharp crack and then a rasping sound as she slid them downward.

She gave a low rumble.

"Let's go," she said.

Odon, the youngest of the elephants, walked very close to Silver Tusk, his mother. He pressed her leg and put his trunk in his mouth. Baby elephants suck trunks instead of thumbs. Ana, his six-year-old sister, walked beside him. She touched him lovingly, and he took his trunk out of his mouth. Cana, his five-year-old cousin, walked behind Odon. She touched him frequently. All the young females adored Odon. He was a baby elephant prince.

He was also a frightened prince. His mother was in a strange mood. She did not stop walking to nurse him. She did not pause to embrace him or even to let him rest. She walked slowly but with urgency. All the Wamba elephants walked slowly but with urgency.

Odon tripped over his awkward trunk and fell. His mother stopped. She put one foot under his body, reached across him, and pulled him to his feet with her trunk. Ana blew the dirt off his head. Cana showed him how to carry his long nose curled toward his chin. Would he ever grow up and learn to master this nose of his? His mother could pick up a tiny seed with her trunk. Ana could dig holes with hers. Odon only tripped on his trunk.

The elephants stopped to eat creeping herbs, then walked on.

The scent of a herd of bull elephants was on the wind. Odon shuddered at the power of their odor. The huge bulls lived by themselves. Among them was Odon's father. Odon would join him when he was twelve years old. Now he knew only loving females and young, tough males who wrestled and butted each other.

The silent Wambas came to a field of tasty green grass. Silver Tusk did not stop. No one stopped. Ana reached out, grabbed a clump of luscious grass with her trunk, and yanked it up by the roots. She knocked off the excess dirt against her back and stuffed the grass in her mouth, all without losing her stride.

At noon they came to a swamp surrounding a muddy lake. Zebras retreated before them. Crowned cranes flew up and away. Silver Tusk left Odon with Ana and waded into the cool mud. She sprayed muddy water, rolled, and wallowed in the mud.

Ana took Odon into the mud. He sprayed, rolled, and wallowed. Mud was ecstasy. Was mud what Silver Tusk was walking to find?

Apparently not. His mother lifted her trunk and sniffed the air.

She flapped her ears, which made a sharp crack, and then she rumbled, "Let's go."

Odon stopped. He had mud in his nose. This nose was such a nuisance.

His mother cleaned it out and they moved swiftly on.

They came to a dust hole. With their trunks, they picked up snoutfuls and blew them over their backs and heads. Silver Tusk stood still to let Odon nurse. Then she gently powdered him with dust. Dust was ecstasy. Was this what Silver Tusk was walking so urgently to find?

Apparently not. Silver Tusk lifted her trunk and flapped her ears. She rumbled, and the Wambas walked on.

She walked past antelope. They stood back. A herd of wildebeest moved out of her way.

Odon discovered a guinea fowl. He swished his trunk and blew air at her. She squawked and flew. He lifted his trunk to his left eye and admired it. It wasn't so bad after all. It could send a bird flying away.

Odon carried his trunk a little bit higher.

Hours later, Silver Tusk stopped. She flapped her ears and held them out like barn doors. She rumbled so piercingly that Odon hid under her. A clear scented liquid poured like tears from her temple glands. It filled the air with messages of who and where and what.

From a distance came an answering rumble. Odon wrapped his trunk around his mother's knee.

Wise Tembo, the matriarch of the Nimbas, had answered Silver Tusk. Her temple glands flowed.

"Run!" Silver Tusk rumbled to the Wambas.

"Run!" Wise Tembo rumbled to the Nimbas.

Both families ran. The earth trembled. Trees shook. Birds flew.

Odon ran beneath his mother.

Silver Tusk and Wise Tembo came together. They lifted their heads and clicked tusks. They twined trunks and embraced. The other elephants, young and old, lifted heads and clicked tusks, screamed and trumpeted.

"Hello, cousins," they were saying.

Wise Tembo reached down to touch and admire Odon. He was not afraid of her. She smelled like his mother.

Slowly Odon lifted his little trunk, held out his ears, and greeted his mother's sister. Silver Tusk had walked all day to find her.

Then the fun began.

Ana pulled a tree up by the roots. She ran in a circle with it.

Young Nimba males and females chased her. They piled on top of one another. They pushed their heads together. They plucked up clumps of tall grass and threw them at each other. All the elephants trumpeted.

Odon wanted to join the joyful family reunion. But he couldn't. His trunk got in his way. Angrily he whipped it toward the ground. To his great surprise, it fell on a stick. He picked it up. He waved it. All the elephants trumpeted and flapped their ears in praise of him.

Odon sat down. He had had a big day. He had learned that mud was splendid, dust was lovely, and an elephant reunion was fun.

But best of all he had learned how to use his nose. As of today he was truly an elephant.

Elephant Talk

in posture and sound

HELLO.
Trunk-twining, touching, embracing.

WE ARE WITH YOU.
Lifting a fallen herd member.
(Shows compassion.)

LET'S GO.
Ears are lifted out,
then drawn down
across neck with
scratching sound.

WATCH OUT.
I'M DANGEROUS.
Head and tail raised.
Ears spread, trunk
hanging. Also nod-
ding with ears half
spread while
approaching a herd
member.

HOW EXCITING! *also*
HOW TERRIBLE!
Flowing temporal
glands.

I'M COMING AT YOU!
Rapid approach,
ears spread, head
high, tail out.
Growling, roaring,
trumpeting,
screaming.

WHO IS BOSS?
Heads raised, tusks or trunk bases meeting. The one standing the tallest is boss.

I LOVE YOU, MOMMY.
Holds mother's tail. Squeals in distress. Puts trunk in mother's mouth.

I'M A HUMBLE ELEPHANT.
Turning away and backing up. Ears flattened, back arching, tail raised.

A PREDATOR IS HERE.
Head raised, ears spread. Tail raised, trunk raised or sniffing. Herd forms ring around calves.

WATCH OUT!
Trumpeting, screaming, growling, roaring.

I LOVE YOU, BABY.
Frequent touching with trunk and feet. Helping calf to feet, using one foot and trunk. Crooking trunk around rump to boost up places. Pushing calf under her in hot sun or danger. Spraying with water and scrubbing gently with trunk. Steering calf by holding its tail.

Disney is committed to wildlife conservation worldwide. At Disney's
Animal Kingdom, most of the animals that guests will see were born in
zoological parks. A safari adventure ride features live animals in a
re-creation of the African savanna. Guests can also visit Conservation
Station, the headquarters for conservation and species survival activities.

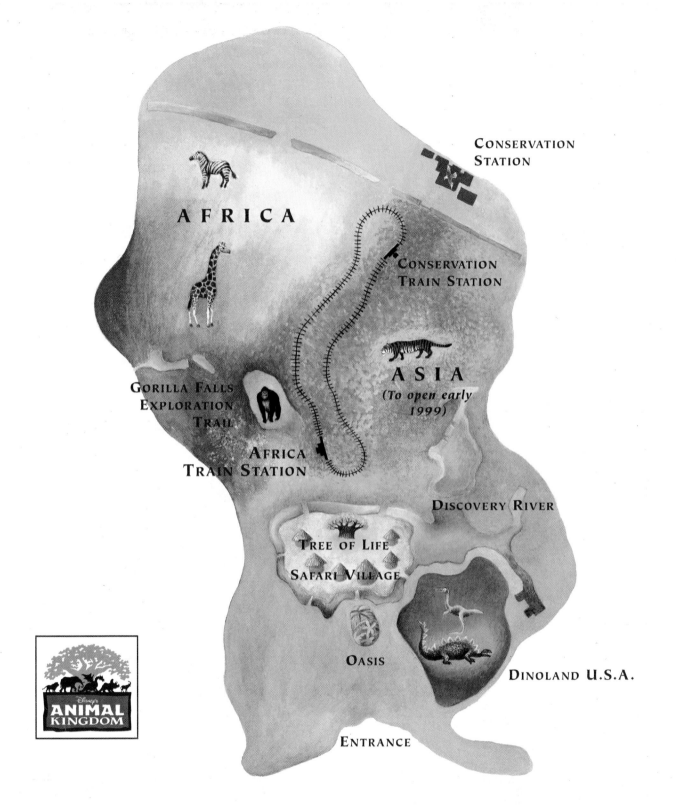

CONSERVATION STATION

AFRICA

CONSERVATION TRAIN STATION

ASIA
(To open early 1999)

GORILLA FALLS EXPLORATION TRAIL

AFRICA TRAIN STATION

DISCOVERY RIVER

TREE OF LIFE

SAFARI VILLAGE

OASIS

DINOLAND U.S.A.

ENTRANCE

Disney's
ANIMAL KINGDOM

To Anna Patricia—J.C.G.

To Prokop—A.V.

Text © 1998 by Jean Craighead George
Illustrations © 1998 by Anna Vojtech

Printed in the United States of America.

First Edition
1 3 5 7 9 10 8 6 4 2

The artwork for each picture is prepared using watercolor.
The book is set in 16-point Tiepolo Bold.
Designed by Stephanie Bart-Horvath
Library of Congress Cataloging-in-Publication Number: 97-80425
ISBN: 0-7868-3163-4

For more Disney Press fun, visit www.Disney Books.com